Is That WISE, Pig?

by
Jan Thomas

BEACH LANE BOOKS • New York London Toronto Sydney New Delhi

Who wants to help me make soup?

I do!

Here is ONE onion!

Here are TWO cabbages!
And here are . . .

THREE
umbrellas!

Three umbrellas?
In the soup?

Is that WISE, Pig?

Oh.
I guess not.

Now here are FOUR tomatoes!

Here are **FIVE** potatoes!
And here are . . .

SIX
galoshes!

SIX GALOSHES?
IN THE SOUP?

Is that WISE, Pig?

Oh.
I guess not.

Now here are SEVEN green beans!

Here are EIGHT Brussels sprouts!
And here are . . .

NINE carrots!
YES!!!
Pretty wise, huh?

And . . .

I asked TEN hungry friends to join us!

Was **THAT** **WISE**, Pig?

Uh-oh!
Better use these!

The umbrellas and galoshes were pretty wise, Pig.
Thanks, Cow.

There's just one thing missing. . . .

Really? What's that, Pig?

ME!!!!

Pizza?
PIZZA!